Father Fox's
Feast of Songs

This book is dedicated to
Julian Ames Devlin

Father Fox's
Feast of Songs

Words and Music by Clyde Watson

Pictures by Wendy Watson

Wordsong
Boyds Mills Press

Published by Wordsong
Boyds Mills Press, Inc.
A Highlights Company
910 Church Street
Honesdale, Pennsylvania 18431
Originally published by Philomel Books, a division of The Putnam Publishing Group,
New York, 1983.
Publisher Cataloging-in-Publication Data
Watson, Clyde.
Father fox's feast of songs / words and music by Clyde Watson ; pictures by Wendy Watson.
[32] p. : col. ill. ; cm.
Originally published by Philomel Books, New York, 1983.
Summary: Twenty-one poems in the style of traditional nursery rhymes, selected from the
author's two earlier collections, with original
musical settings for family singing.
ISBN 1-878093-84-3
1. Children's songs—United States. [1. Songs] I. Watson, Wendy, ill.
II. Title.
782.42—dc20   1992
Library of Congress Catalog Card Number 91-67935
Distributed by St. Martin's Press
Printed in Hong Kong

10 9 8 7 6 5 4 3 2 1

Contents

Here's a Song

Sweetly

Here's a song of Tin-ker and Pe - ter, Hon-ey is sweet but love is sweet-er—

What comes next now tell me dear - ly, Al - ex - an - der dar - ling.

Butterprint

Flowing

But-ter-print knocks at the milk-shop door___ What will he have to-day, ___ A rose-bud, a dump-ling, a nip-per-kin of milk, then But-ter-print's on his way.

Pig Song

Oh, My Goodness!

Punchy

Oh my good-ness, oh my dear,_ Sas - sa - fras and gin-ger beer,_ Choc-'late cake and ap - ple punch:_ I'm too full to eat my lunch, too full to eat my_ lunch.

Huckleberry, Gooseberry

Dilly Dilly

With pep

Dil - ly Dil - ly Pic - a - lil - li, Tell me, tell me some-thing ver-y sil - ly, ver-y sil-ly:＿ Well, there

was a chap, his name was Bert,＿ He ate the but-tons, ate the but-tons, ate the but-tons off his   shirt, off his shirt!

Piggy
Back
Song

Old Tin Cup

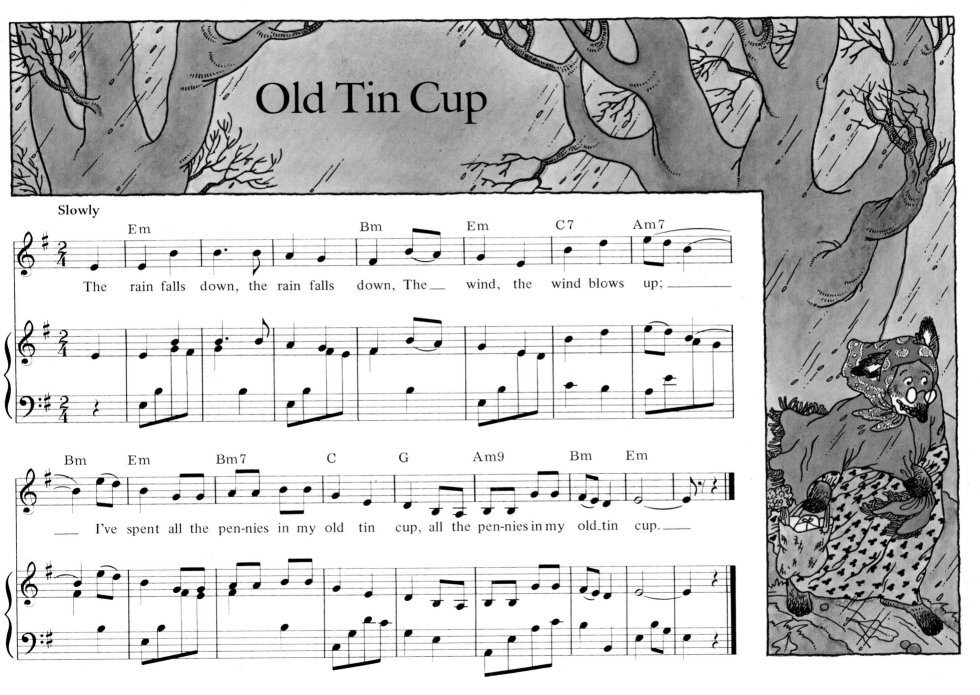

Slowly

The rain falls down, the rain falls down, The___ wind, the wind blows up;___

___ I've spent all the pen-nies in my old tin cup, all the pen-nies in my old tin cup.___

The Baby Cakewalk

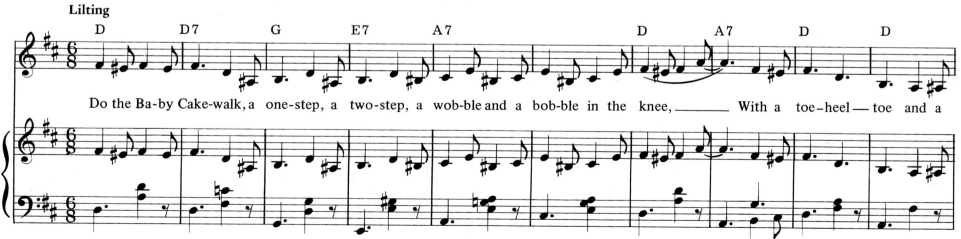

Do the Ba-by Cake-walk, a one-step, a two-step, a wob-ble and a bob-ble in the knee, _____ With a toe–heel—toe and a

gid-dy-go-round you go, Won't you do the Ba-by Cake-walk for me?___ me?_____

Hushabye

Belly & Tubs

Rollicking

D

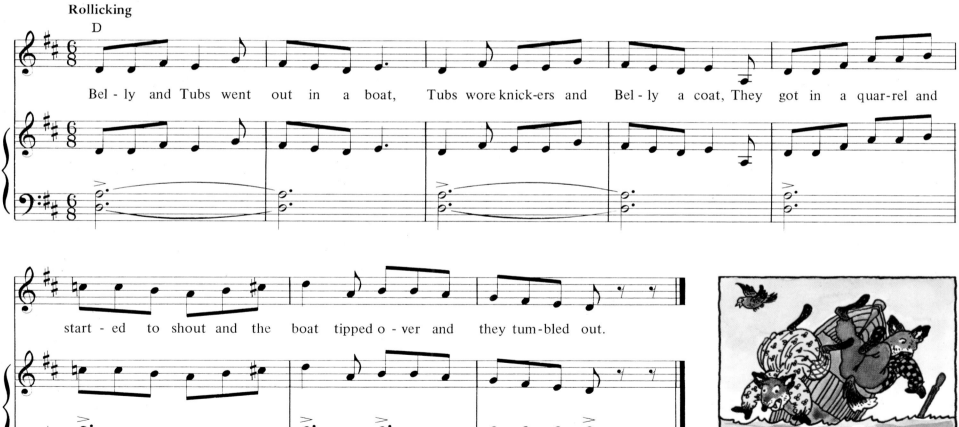

Bel - ly and Tubs went out in a boat, Tubs wore knick-ers and Bel - ly a coat, They got in a quar-rel and

start - ed to shout and the boat tipped o - ver and they tum-bled out.

Bimbo Bombo

Swinging blues

Bim - bo Bom - bo_ Tom - kin Pie,_ He is the ap - ple_ of my eye._

S-wing him low__ S-wing him high _ He is the ap - ple of my eye.

20

Ride Your Red Horse

Lullabye

Softly

Rock, rock, sleep, my ba - by, sleep the whole night through.
Hush, hush, sleep, my ba - by, sings the sweet cuck - oo.

When your dad - dy comes back home he'll bring a toy for you. _____
When your dad - dy comes back home he'll sing a song for you. _____

Mister Lister

See Saw

Rocking

See - saw, Jump - in - the - straw, Give me a bone for my good dog to gnaw.

See - saw, Jump - in - the - straw, If I were a don - key I'd cry, "Hee-haw!"

Miss Quiss

Saucy and quick

Miss Quiss! Look at this! A pock-et full of lic-or-ice! You may have some

If you wish, But ev-'ry stick will cost a kiss! kiss!

Down Derry Down

Uptown, Downtown

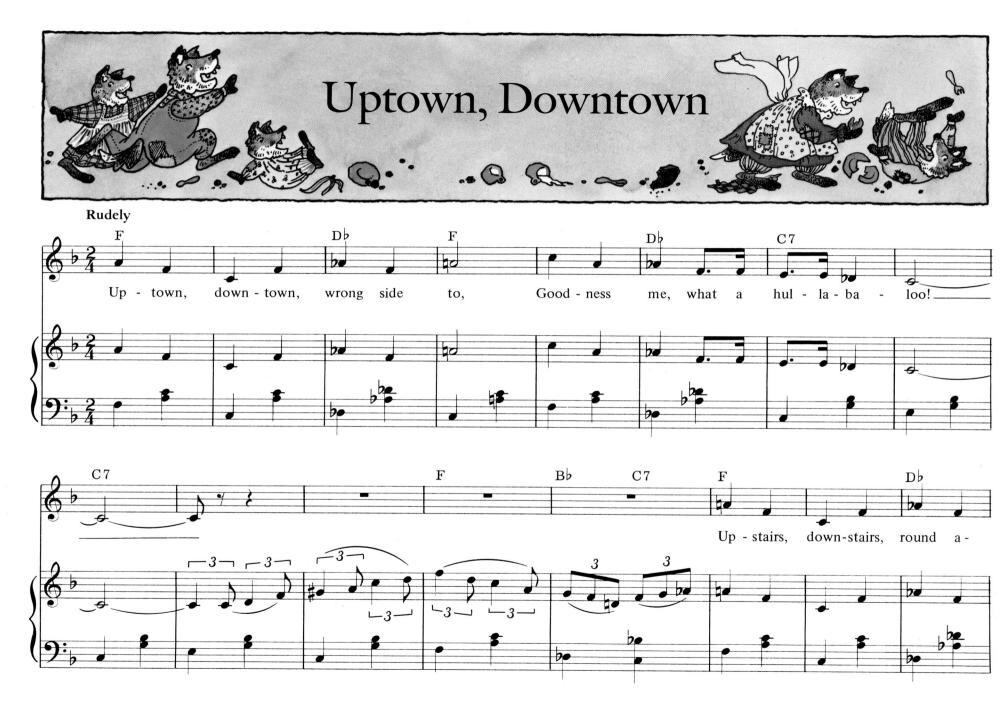

Rudely

Up - town, down - town, wrong side to, Good - ness me, what a hul - la - ba - loo!

Up - stairs, down-stairs, round a -

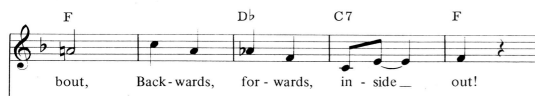

bout,   Back - wards,   for - wards,   in - side ___   out!

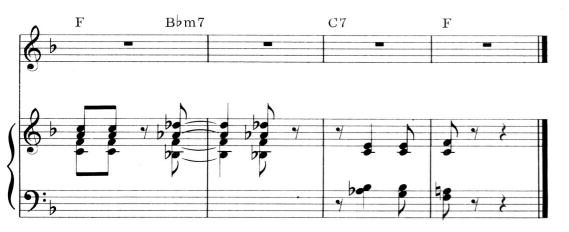

Soft Falls the Snow

Slowly

Soft falls the snow, the coals burn low, _____ Lit-tle Ja-cob's a - sleep on my knee; _____ My

sto-ry ends here _____ For mid-night is near: To bed now, one, two, ___ three! _____

Clyde and Wendy Watson are sisters. Their first collaboration, *Father Fox's Pennyrhymes,*
was hailed as a modern American classic, and its companion book *Catch Me & Kiss Me & Say
It Again* was equally popular. "Alternatives to Ms. Goose, these Mother Watson rhymes
flow through . . . family activities with soft humor, natural as unprocessed honey,"
said *School Library Journal,* and *Publishers Weekly* commented that "all the songs
are the kinds children like to chant." *Clyde Watson* is the author of
many books for children, including *Father Fox's Pennyrhymes.* She and
her family live in Hanover, New Hampshire. *Wendy Watson*
has illustrated more than seventy books, some of which she
has written herself. Her pictures for this book are done
in a combination of pen and ink and watercolor.
With her husband and two children, Miss
Watson lives in Topsham, Vermont.